ANITA'S NATIONAL PARK CLEANUP

CARING FOR OUR EARTH

By
Krystine Cabrera

Illustrated by
Guilherme Salomon

Published by Krystine Cabrera 2023

Anita's National Park Cleanup
Copyright © 2023 by Krystine Cabrera
Cover by Guilherme Salomon

Printed in the USA.
All rights reserved.
No part of this book may be reproduced, transmitted, or stored by any means, electronic, mechanical, photocopying, recording, or otherwise, without written permission from the author. For information regarding permission, all inquiries should be directed to
www.storiesbykrystine.com

ISBN-13: 979-8-9875454-1-6 (Hardcover)
ISBN-13: 979-8-9875454-0-9 (Paperback)

THIS BOOK IS DEDICATED TO MY MATERNAL GRANDPARENTS
AND MY LOVED ONES.

THANK YOU TO ALL THE LITTLE ONES THAT ARE LOOKING TO MAKE
A DIFFERENCE IN THE WORLD.

-KRYSTINE

Hi there! This is Anita, a Junior Park Ranger. Her duty is to protect nature and the animals living here.

"Come on, everybody! Let's enjoy the park together and help make it a safe place to play and have some fun!"

Anita was planning a scavenger hunt for her friends. She couldn't wait to explore the park with them.

Maybe they would
even discover a few
pretty birds, find leaves with all sorts of
colors, and see some squirrels climbing
on trees.

But when Anita came to the campgrounds, she couldn't believe her eyes. Instead of singing birds, beautiful flowers, and lush green trees, she saw nothing but trash.

There were plastic bottles everywhere, cans were all over the ground, and she even saw a deer holding a bag of chips.

Anita rushed towards the headquarters
of the Junior Park Rangers and saw her
friends, Richard and Jasmin.

"You won't believe this," she said, all out
of breath, "there's trash everywhere!"

Together, the kids each grabbed a pair of reusable cleanup gloves, the big kind that reaches to the elbow, keeping their hands clean and safe.

"How did all this trash get here?" Anita asked.

"No way!" Richard frowned. "There's still so much to clean here!"

"But what can we do?"
Anita asked. "A fun
scavenger hunt could help
get more kids to care
about the park and the
animals."

"I know," Richard agreed,
"but we can always have
our scavenger hunt later."

Jasmin frowned, "But not
if we don't get extra help
with the cleanup first."

Anita had an idea. "I know!"
she exclaimed. "We can have
a TRASH scavenger hunt.
That way, all the kids and
their parents can help us
with the cleanup WHILE
learning to care about our
park at the same time!"

Richard smiled, "Good idea!
We could clean the park
faster and be able to
enjoy nature together!"

"Let's do it! That'll be a fun
game!" Jasmin said with
excitement.

So, Anita got to work. She talked to kids and their parents and invited other people in the community to the park.

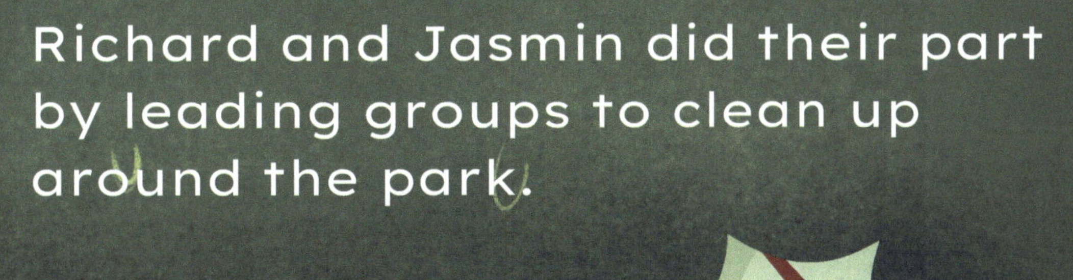

Richard and Jasmin did their part by leading groups to clean up around the park.

"Look at this!" a boy
named Dylan called out.
"I found a doll!"

"And I found a stylish
pair of sunglasses!" a
girl named Alex
excitedly stated.

"Wow! These items don't look like trash," Richard said, confused.

"Leaving things behind is littering, even if it's accidental," Jasmin explained.

"Oh no!" Anita cried. "That bird is stuck in the trash! It can't fly!"

A poor little bird was caught in a plastic ring used to hold soda together.

"Help!" Anita yelled.

Together, the kids tried to remove the plastic ring by hand, but it just wouldn't come off.

"The ring is too tight on the bird," Jasmin cried.

"I am afraid of hurting it if I pull too hard," Richard frowned, gently holding the bird in his hands.

"We can help!" said Alex, holding a pair of scissors.

Dylan carefully pulled up the plastic ring, and Alex cut it.

"There you are, little friend!" Dylan said to the bird as the ring loosened and fell to the ground.

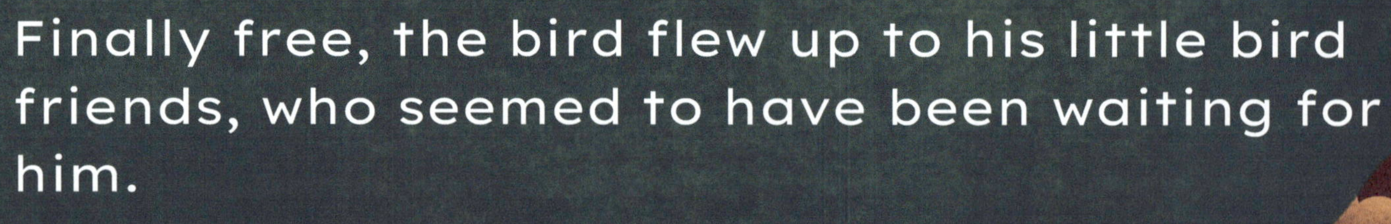

Finally free, the bird flew up to his little bird friends, who seemed to have been waiting for him.

"Look at the bird go!" Dylan said, excitedly.

"Be free, my friend!" Alex cheered.
"Freedom!" Anita shouted.
"Wow! We did it!" Richard said in awe.
"Listen to the birds sing happily!" Jasmin
smiled.

The friends continued to clean up the campgrounds, picking up all the trash they could find.

"I don't want another animal hurt by this trash," Anita said.

"But how can we prevent this?" Dylan asked.

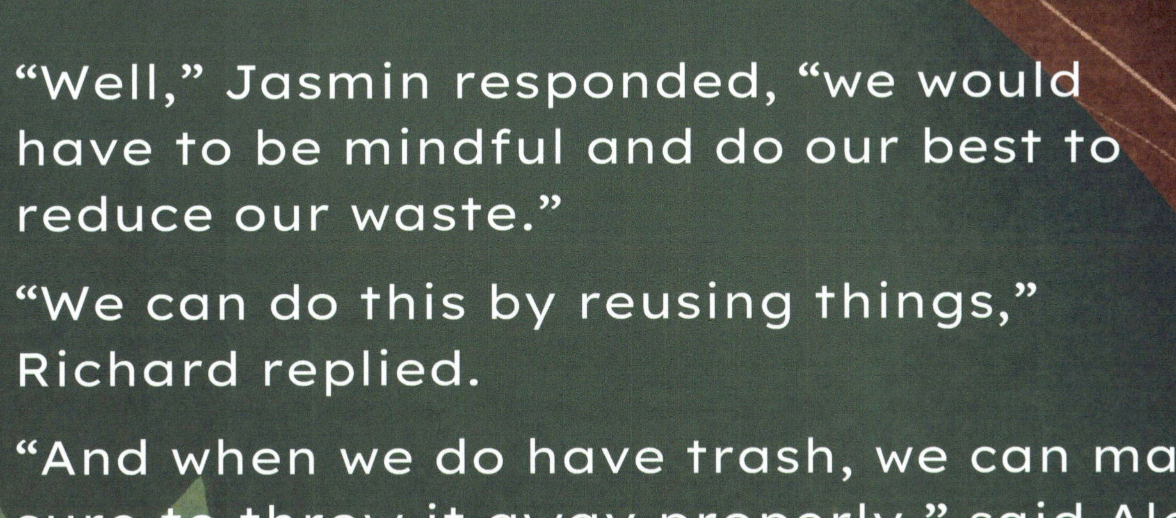

"Well," Jasmin responded, "we would have to be mindful and do our best to reduce our waste."

"We can do this by reusing things," Richard replied.

"And when we do have trash, we can make sure to throw it away properly," said Alex.

"I have some exciting news!" Anita shared at the end of the day. "With the help of Dylan and Alex, our park is clean again, and all of our animals are safe. I am happy to announce that they are our newest Junior Park Rangers!"

Everyone applauded as Anita handed their badges to them. As everyone cheered, Dylan and Alex raised their right hand and promised to protect, respect, and appreciate the land and animals.

"This is just the beginning!" Anita beamed. "Together, we can make the world a better place!"

GLOSSARY

<u>Campgrounds</u>: an outdoor place where people camp using a tent or other shelter.

<u>Headquarters</u>: the main place or office of an organization or group.

<u>Junior Park Rangers</u>: a program for young children who pledge to learn, explore, and protect National Parks and their resources.

<u>Littering</u>: the act of leaving trash or objects behind in places that they do not belong.

<u>Scavenger Hunt</u>: a game for people to look for different items.

<u>Trash</u>: an item that is unwanted or no longer able to use that is thrown away.

IF YOU LIKED THIS BOOK, READ THIS!

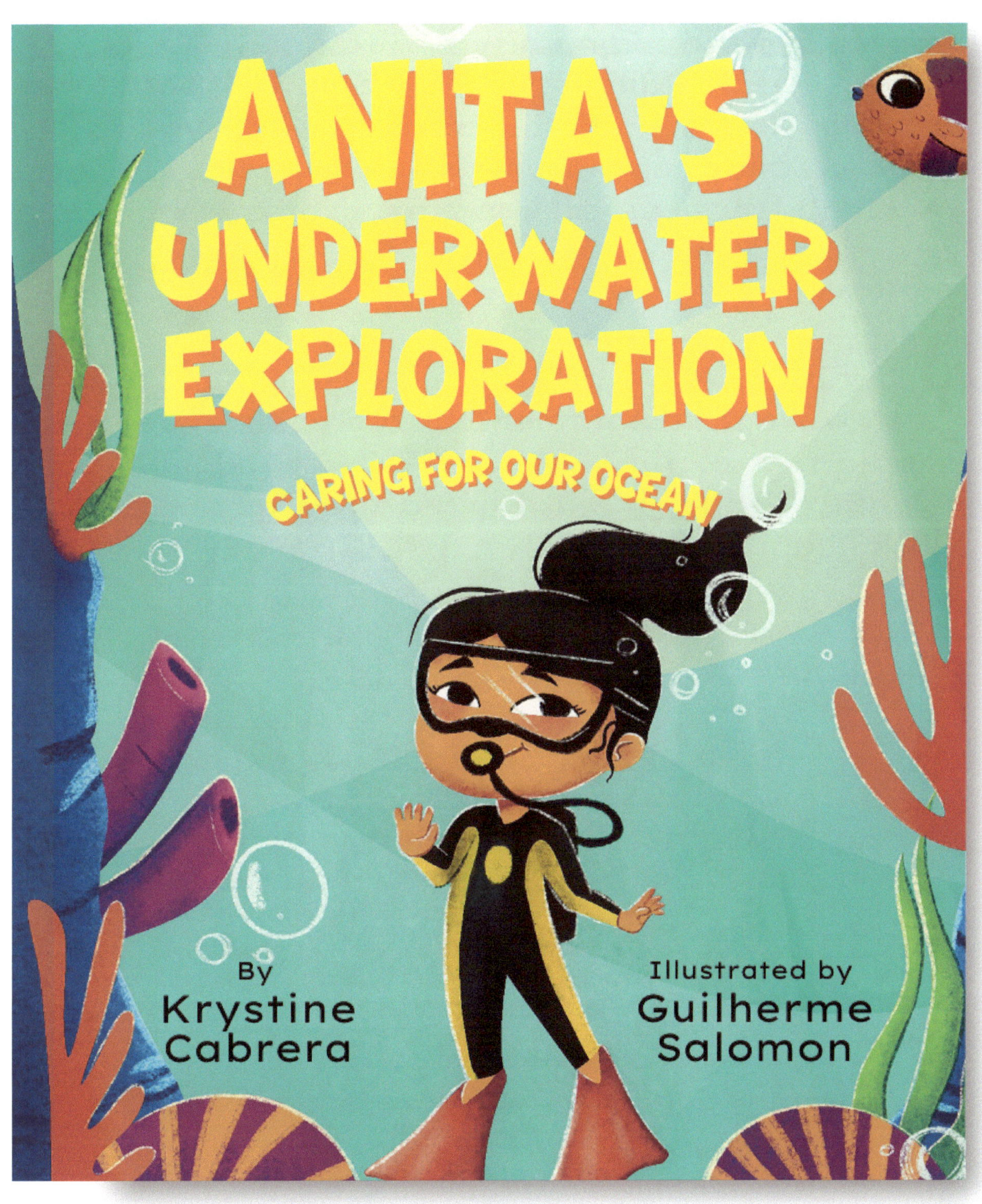

WANT TO GET INVOLVED?

Are you looking for ways to make a positive impact in your community? Anita and her team of Junior Park Rangers have created engaging activity sheets that you can use when you're on your cleanup adventures. These resources are available for free at www.storiesbykrystine.com, and they are filled with fun and engaging activities!

In addition, Anita offers an exciting opportunity to show your commitment to the environment. By sending a picture of yourself practicing eco-friendly habits, it will be featured in the Junior Park Rangers' exclusive HALL OF FAME. This feature is a great way to motivate others and display your efforts. The process is simple; send the picture via email to:

hello@storiesbykrystine.com

Taking care of our environment is important, and we're so glad you're part of it!

ABOUT THE AUTHOR

Krystine Cabrera was born in Seattle and raised by her Filipino father and half-Filipino, half-Caucasian mother, who instilled in her a passion for education. As a child, Krystine was an avid reader and enjoyed crafting stories of her own.

Drawing on her personal experiences, Krystine now writes to motivate and empower young readers to positively impact their lives and the world. Her latest work aims to inspire parents to involve their children in litter cleanup efforts, hoping to create a cleaner and healthier planet.

ACKNOWLEDGEMENTS

I want to express my gratitude to Yvonne (Eevi) Jones for her invaluable guidance in creating this book. Eevi read my manuscript and gave so much feedback for the book to be the way it is today! She also had useful tips that helped me achieve a successful book launch. Additionally, my parents and sisters have been incredibly supportive throughout this process by sharing my book with their friends and colleagues. I would also like to thank Jasmin Williams, Bryton Martin, and Terra Hoy for their unwavering support over the years through my most difficult times and for cheering me on during this writing process. Lastly, I appreciate Dave Bodach, my former math teacher, whose Volunteer Club inspired me to start picking up litter to better the environment. In 2022, I planned cleanups where we picked up a total of 1,884 pounds of litter!